IDA
AND THE
WHALE

REBECCA·GUGGER
SIMON RÖTHLISBERGER

North
South

THERE

was once a little girl named
Ida, who lived in a birch tree.
She had yellow rubber boots
and red hair.

Ida often sat high up outside
her tree house, wondering what
lay beyond the sun, the moon,
and the stars.

One night, the tree house suddenly began to S H A K E.

It shook so hard that her bed began to slide here, there, and everywhere.

What was happening?

WOW!

Outside was a gigantic

F L Y I N G

WHALE.

"Why are you waking
me in the middle of
the night?" asked Ida,
still half asleep.

"Would you like to come with me on a journey beyond the stars?" asked the friendly whale. What an adventure! Of course Ida wanted to go with him. In a flash she had climbed the ladder . . .

. . . and then the two of them flew
up and up toward the world

BEYOND . . .

As they flew through the
middle of a thick curtain of clouds
they talked about all kinds of things.
BIG and little.
Ordinary and S P E C I A L.
Known and unknown.

They soon reached a very strange place. Everything seemed to be UPSIDE DOWN. What was the top and what was the bottom?

"So now what is NORMAL?" asked the whale. "Sometimes you can only understand others if you stand on your head yourself."

They flew upside down until
they came to a beautiful green
place that was full of sweet scents.

"Why is the flower flying away?"
asked Ida. "So that it can grow again–
like the rest of us," said the whale.
"Some quicker, some slower.
But all of us

GROW."

Suddenly thunder rumbled
softly but then it became louder and
LOUDER.
More and more clouds began to pile up,
and dazzling flashes of lightning shot
out of them. The storm was wild and
violent, and left nothing untouched.
"I'm glad there are two of us,"
thought Ida.

Slowly the storm calmed down. And then everything was still and empty.

"Just wait and then look again," said the whale. "Sometimes there's

Ida looked around.

more to see than you think."

Ida listened to the silence for quite a
while. And suddenly she felt lonely and
a long way from home. She was so small
and so alone.

Where was her

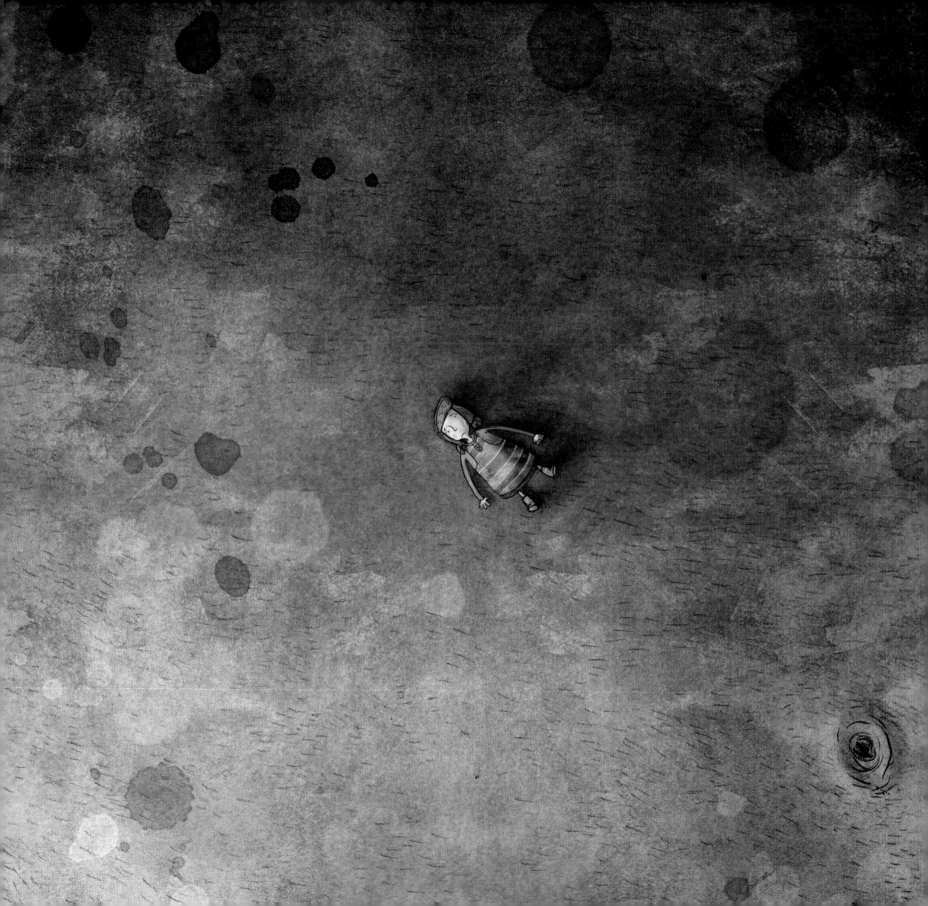

The whale gave Ida a nudge.

"Why are you so sad, my little friend?"
he asked. "I'm right here. Sometimes it's nice
to share a silence. Sometimes you can even lose
sight of each other. But you're still close
together–always!" Ida's loneliness flew

F A R   A W A Y.

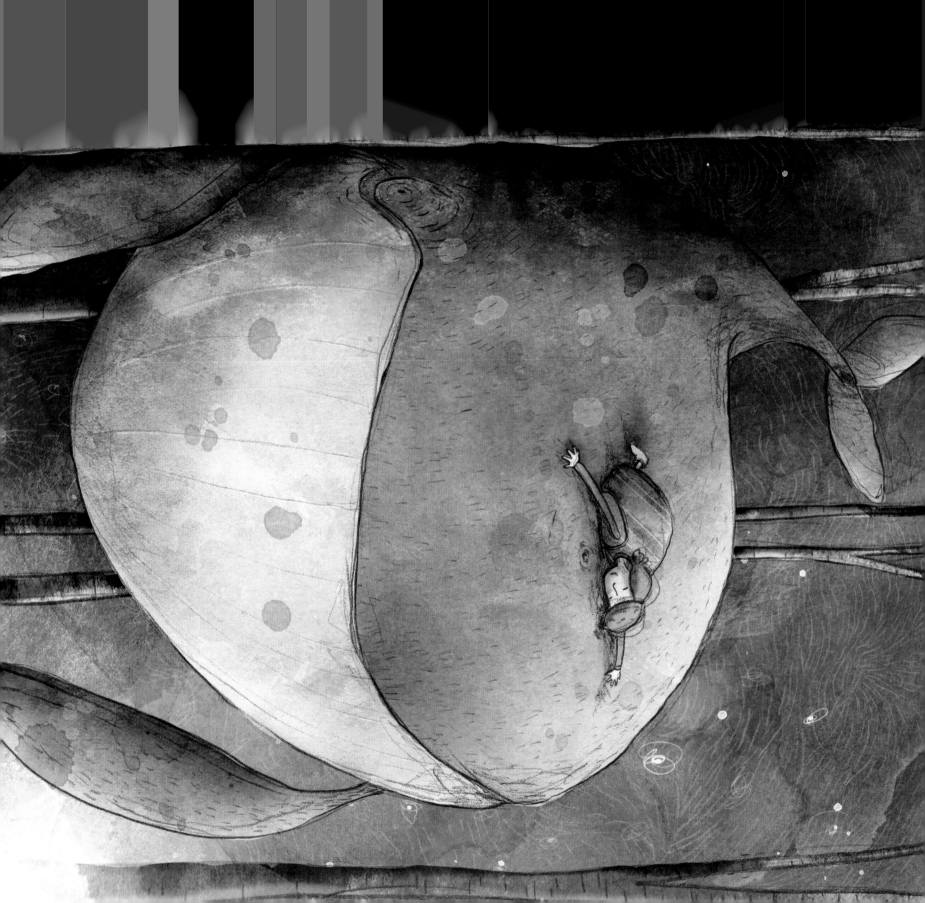

"I love you, my flying
G I A N T,"
whispered Ida as the two of them
said good-bye. "See you soon!"
they shouted to each other.
And the whale disappeared
behind the trees.

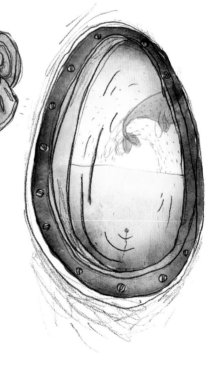

STORM

FRIEND

Rebecca Gugger (b. 1983) and **Simon Röthlisberger** (b. 1984) were both born in Switzerland and live together in Thun, close to the forests, the mountains, and the fresh air.

Rebecca is a freelance illustrator and graphic artist, studied at the HKB (Bern University of the Arts), and likes to have her head in the clouds. Simon is a trained graphic artist, is currently working as an art director, and likes sailing.

Now and again the two of them work together, with pen and with paint.

Copyright © 2018 by NordSüd Verlag AG, CH-8050 Zürich, Switzerland.

First published in Switzerland under the title *Ida und der fliegende Wal*.

English translation copyright © 2018 by NorthSouth Books, Inc., New York 10016. Translated by David Henry Wilson.

First published in the United States and Canada in 2018 by NorthSouth Books, Inc., an imprint of NordSüd Verlag AG, CH-8050 Zürich, Switzerland.

Distributed in the United States by NorthSouth Books, Inc., New York 10016. Library of Congress Cataloging-in-Publication Data is available.

ISBN: 978-0-7358-4341-7
Printed in Latvia by Livonia Print, Riga, 2018.
1 3 5 7 9 • 10 8 6 4 2

www.northsouth.com

MIX
Paper from responsible sources
FSC® C002795